THE SECRET OF SHERLOCK HOLMES

by
Jeremy Paul

PLAYERS PRESS, Inc.
P.O. Box 1132
Studio City, CA 91614-0132

THE SECRET OF SHERLOCK HOLMES

© Copyright, 1989, 1991 and 1996, by Jeremy Paul
and Players Press, Inc.
U.K. ISBN 0-86025-438-0
U.S. ISBN 0-88734-708-8
Library of Congress Catalogue Number: 96-36105

ALL RIGHTS RESERVED

CAUTION: Professionals and amateurs are hereby warned that this play being fully protected under the copyright laws of the United States of America, the British Commonwealth, including the Dominion of Canada, and all other countries of the Copyright Union, is subject to a royalty. All rights, including stock, amateur, motion pictures, recitation, public reading, radio broadcast, television, and the rights of translation into foreign languages are strictly reserved. In its present form the play is dedicated to the reading public only.

This play may be presented by amateurs upon payment of a royalty for each performance, payable to Players Press, Inc., P.O. Box 1132, Studio City, CA 91614-0132, U.S.A.

Professional royalty quoted on application to Players Press.

Particular emphasis is laid on the question of amateur or professional readings and cuttings, permission for which must be secured in writing from Players Press.

Copying from this book in whole or part is strictly forbidden by law, and the right of performance is not transferable.

Whenever the play is produced the following notice must appear on all programs, printing and advertising for the play:

"Produced by special arrangement with Players Press."

Due authorship credit must be given on all programs, printing and advertising for the play.

Simultaneously Published
U.S.A., U.K., Canada and Australia

Printed in the U.S.A.

Library of Congress Cataloging-in-Publication Data

Paul, Jeremy.
　The secret of Sherlock Holmes / by Jeremy Paul.
　　p.　cm.
　ISBN 0-88734-708-8 (alk. paper)
　1. Holmes, Sherlock (Fictitious character)--Drama.　I. Title.
PR6066.A882S43　1996
822'.914--dc20
　　　　　　　　　　　　　　　　　　　　　　　　　　　　96-36105
　　　　　　　　　　　　　　　　　　　　　　　　　　　　CIP

THE SECRET OF SHERLOCK HOLMES

INTRODUCTION

'The circumstances which led to my first meeting with Sherlock Holmes - a meeting which was to change and shape my life - are of no consequence, except to say...'

Watson's opening lines in the play are ringing in my head as I begin this introduction. It's rather unnerving to confront a genius and discover that he might also become a friend and one might have a role to play in his life. Like Watson, I have become a chronicler, a sort of latterday Boswell, for that most elusive and beguiling of heroes. I had read the canon as a schoolboy, but in no sense could I claim to be a Sherlockian or a Doylian. The stories had registered, but not deeply. I was rusticating somewhere in the country when Michael Cox called from Granada Television, inviting me to join a team of writers to adapt the original stories for the small screen. The brief was 'get back to Conan Doyle', to be as faithful as possible and, in particular, to set the record straight about the character of Watson. Spoofing was out.

I started with *The Speckled Band*. The story was so beautifully structured for an hour's television that I scarcely had to tinker with it at all. *The Naval Treaty* was a tougher nut. *The Musgrave Ritual* needed complete restructuring and my fourth attempt, *Wisteria Lodge*, was so obdurate that it took longer to write than the stage play. I felt there were so many people out there, so many real devotees who might be grieved by the liberties we often had to take to fit the hour's formula. But the ship was steadied by another kind of devotion from a superb and caring production team, design, costume, camera work and the inspired casting of Jeremy Brett as Holmes and, first, David Burke and then Edward Hardwicke as Watson.

'It was in the summer of '87 that the idea first came to me...' And it came about in this fashion. Jeremy reminded me that it was Holmes' centenary and we ought to do something about it. A celebratory evening in a theatre: extracts from the canon, a reading, a birthday present anyway. The challenge triggered off something that must have been burrowing away in my subconscious. While doing the adaptations, I found myself more and more fascinated by the **beginnings** of the stories wherein lay this extraordinary, detailed Victorian friendship between two men which carried no modern sexual overtones at all.

Just friendship, uncomplicated in its nature, something that perhaps our hurrying world has lost sight of. Added to this was Conan Doyle's sharp insight into the social and moral climate of his times. So often these openings had to be skimmed in the television versions, in order to move quickly into the narrative of the 'case'. It was like stumbling across a trunkful of treasures in an attic and it is possible that Conan Doyle himself was unaware of their value. He was often self-deprecating about his talents.

I told Jeremy that I wanted to write a play about Holmes and Watson, based on Conan Doyle's own words. Entranced, but perhaps a little wary, Jeremy commissioned it, and I plunged headlong down what I knew was a thorny and well-trodden path. I didn't care. I plundered the canon for bits from this story and that, discovering along the way Conan Doyle's marvellous ear for theatrical language and humour. And I had another bonus. I was able to tap Jeremy's own knowledge of Holmes through a series of tapes he made, gleaned from five years of playing the part. Brilliantly he filled in gaps, such as the mystery of Holmes' unrecorded childhood (an actor has to resolve these things), or his inner feelings, for instance, about **the** woman, Irene Adler (an actor can still catch the fragrance of an actress's scent). The tapes were to prove invaluable.

But if this was to be a play about friendship, there was a mystery to solve. How could any man allow his closest friend to believe he was dead for three whole years? Therein lay the enigma and the key to Holmes' complex personality. If I could unravel that...

The 'secret' of Holmes and Moriarty presented itself as something so thrilling and, at the same time, so obvious that I thought it must have been explored many times, if only as a hypothesis. I checked with a Sherlockian friend who reassured me that I was on (relatively) new ground. It had once been proffered humorously by A G MacDonnell in *Punch* in the thirties, but never followed up. That was good enough for me. After the play opened I learnt that it also forms the basis of *The Last Sherlock Holmes* by Michael Dibdin (Jonathan Cape, 1978): comparisons may be interesting. The fun, anyway, is to stir up a debate, and an enthusiast can always put the 'secret' through its supreme and ultimate test by measuring it against the evidence in the canon.

One other element was important to me, something I remembered from Michael Cox's first briefing – and that was to do justice to Watson's character. A brave soldier who has seen the horrors of war, a general practitioner who understands the complex psychology of human beings, and a man whom his friend describes as 'the one fixed point in a changing world'. I needed Watson to have his day, to play Holmes at his own game and not be found wanting.

As I write this, we are completing a happy and eventful year at the beautiful Wyndham's Theatre in the West End. I have had the great joy of meeting Dame Jean Conan Doyle and seeing a smile on her face. And I've enjoyed many conversations with Sherlockians of all ages from all over the world. For mysterious reasons that can only be ascribed to Conan Doyle's genius, his creation is alive and well in the latter part of the twentieth century, and there is a spring in his stride as he takes on the next hundred years.

As far as this play is concerned, I acknowledge my debt and tip my hat to Jeremy Brett and Edward Hardwicke, to Duncan Weldon and Triumph Theatre Productions for putting it on, to Patrick Garland for his wise and subtle direction, to Poppy Mitchell for her wonderful evocation of Holmes' London and the Reichenbach Falls, to Mark Pritchard's expert lighting, to Nigel Hess for catching the mood so hauntingly with his music, and to all who have contributed in so many ways behind the scenes.

Would Holmes have approved, or his creator? Well, maybe Watson should have the last word on that. 'I shall, as always respect your wishes, Holmes, and select... and hone... and transpose... and omit... and hopefully fulfil the expectations of your adoring public.'

Jeremy Paul
Swanage
August, 1989

THE SECRET OF SHERLOCK HOLMES

Produced by Duncan C Weldon & Jermone Minskoff for Triumph Theatre Productions Ltd. at Wyndham's Theatre, London, on 22nd September, 1988.

Sherlock Holmes	Jeremy Brett
Doctor Watson	Edward Hardwicke

Directed by Patrick Garland

The action takes place in 221b Baker Street, Doctor Watson's surgery and various other parts of London and in Switzerland.

Enquiries about the incidental music
by Nigel Hess
should be directed to
Myra Music, Ltd.
1a Farm Place, London W8 7SX

ACT ONE

A multiple setting that includes HOLMES' rooms in Baker Street and WATSON's consulting rooms, but includes space for other effects. At the curtain rise HOLMES is spotlighted in the darkness playing the violin. He is alone, mysterious. The light fades on HOLMES and WATSON is discovered downstage, addressing the audience. He is wearing outdoor clothes and is loaded up with books.

WATSON The circumstances which led to my first meeting with Sherlock Holmes - a meeting which was to change and shape my life - are of no consequence, except to say that I had been serving as an Army doctor in the Second Afghan War. I was wounded and despatched home in frail health. For nine months I stayed at a private hotel in the Strand, leading a comfortless, meaningless existence and spending as much money as I had, considerably more freely than I ought. So alarming did the state of my finances become that I soon realised that I must either leave the metropolis and rusticate somewhere in the country or make a complete alteration in my style of living. I was without kith or kin to concern me, and therefore I was, I suppose, as free as air.

HOLMES *(from behind him)* Or as free as an Army Pension of eleven shillings and sixpence a day will permit a man to be.

WATSON turns at the interruption and sees HOLMES advancing upon him.

WATSON Holmes...

HOLMES Watson, tell the truth! Or as much of it as your gullible public can digest. We shall

	not skirt round your gallant contribution to that disastrous war...
WATSON	My part in it was insignificant...
HOLMES	Appointed an Assistant Surgeon to the Fifth Northumberland Fusiliers, you arrived in Bombay to find the second Afghan War had broken out. You made your way through the passes, deep into enemy country. Reached Candahar by a miracle. Took up your duties. You were despatched to join the Berkshires just in time for the fatal battle of Maiwand. There you were struck on the shoulder by a Jezail bullet, which shattered the bone and grazed the subclavian artery. You would have fallen into the hands of the murderous Ghazis, but for the devotion and courage shown by your orderly... what was his name?
WATSON	Murray.
HOLMES	Murray, yes... who threw you across a pack-horse and brought you safely to the British lines.
WATSON	It is recorded. I have recorded it.
HOLMES ignores the interruption.	
HOLMES	The phrase you used in your account... to describe the London you found on your return.
WATSON	The phrase...?
HOLMES	Don't you remember? 'That great cesspool into which all the loungers and idlers of the Empire are irresistibly drained.'
WATSON	I said that?
HOLMES	Yes... and since I've never known you to make a dishonest observation in your life, it was the truth. (*Then privately*) The fact is, the man I met in the chemical laboratory at Bart's was exhausted,

penniless and deeply disillusioned. (*To WATSON*) It was Stamford who introduced us?
WATSON Yes. He warned me against you.
HOLMES I can't think why. I scarcely knew the fellow.
WATSON He'd seen you in the dissecting room beating the subjects with a stick... to verify how far bruises may be produced after death.
HOLMES Ah! The enthusiasm of youth! I've always had a passion for definite and exact knowledge.

The scene is now the rooms in Baker Street. A large desk, cluttered with paraphernalia, including the violin, a globe and the Persian slipper (for tobacco) is stage left. Beside it a couch. Behind it a chair. To its right is HOLMES' easy chair. Stage right a large table filled with elaborate chemical equipment, in front of it another easy chair, with a small table beside it. The visible backcloth depicts a Dore engraved image of London houses and back yards. WATSON addresses the audience:

WATSON Holmes was looking for someone to go halves with him in some lodgings he'd found... which were too much for his purse.
HOLMES You don't mind the smell of strong tobacco, I hope.

WATSON turns upstage as HOLMES is offering his rooms in Baker Street - as WATSON's new home.

WATSON I always smoke 'ships' myself.
HOLMES That's good enough. I generally have chemicals about and occasionally do experiments. Would that annoy you?
WATSON By no means.
HOLMES Let me see - what are my other short--comings? That's my chair... (*WATSON*

was about to sit, but remains standing as HOLMES busily clears papers from the other easy chair and the small table.)
I get in the dumps at times and don't open my mouth for days on end. You mustn't think I'm sulky when I do that. Just leave me alone, and I'll soon be all right. What have you to confess to? It's just as well for two fellows to know the worst of one another before they begin living together.
HOLMES now abandons his vague attempt to tidy the room.
WATSON I get up at all sorts of ungodly hours and I'm extremely lazy. And I object to rows because my nerves are shaken.
WATSON lays out his possessions on his table.
HOLMES Do you include the violin in your category of rows?
WATSON It depends on the player. A well-played violin is a treat for the gods... a badly played one...
HOLMES Oh, that's all right then... I think we may consider the thing as settled – if the rooms are agreeable to you. And you can manage the terms.
WATSON Yes, indeed.
HOLMES offers his hand on the deal, almost shyly, as an afterthought. WATSON shakes it warmly. Then removes his coat and hangs it up. A stiffness of shoulder movement can be seen in his actions.
HOLMES You have been in Afghanistan, I perceive.
WATSON *(astonished)* Yes. How the deuce did you know that?
HOLMES My reasoning tells me that here is a gentleman of a medical type, but with the air of a military man. Clearly an army doctor, then. He has just come from the tropics, for his face is dark and that is

     not the natural tint of his skin... for his wrists are fair. He has undergone hardship and sickness. His left arm has been injured. Now, where in the tropics could an English army doctor have seen such hardship and got his arm wounded? Clearly in Afghanistan.
WATSON Excellent!
HOLMES (*dismissively, as he perambulates around his desk and sits in the chair*) No, no, it's elementary. The whole train of thought did not occupy a second.

HOLMES *scans some papers he has recently dumped into the wastepaper basket.*

WATSON But how can you put these powers to use?
HOLMES (*laughs*) My trade is that of a consulting detective. It's how I earn my bread and cheese.
WATSON You remind me of Edgar Allan Poe's Dupin.
HOLMES Dupin...

HOLMES *drops the papers back into the basket and* WATSON *knows at once that he has blundered into a sensitive area.*

HOLMES No doubt you think you're complimenting me. Dupin was a very inferior fellow. That trick of his of breaking in on his friends' thoughts with a clever remark. Very showy and superficial.
WATSON He had some analytical genius.
HOLMES Not half as much as Poe appeared to imagine.
WATSON Have you read Gaboriau's works? Does Lecoq come up to your idea of a detective?
HOLMES (*sniffs sardonically*) Lecoq was a miserable bungler. That book made me positively ill. He took six months to identify

11

an unknown poisoner. I could have done it in twenty-four hours. It might be a textbook for detectives to teach them what to avoid.

WATSON decides on a canny test of HOLMES' deductive powers. He produces a gold pocket-watch on a chain from his files.

WATSON Holmes... would you think me impertinent if I put your gifts to a more severe test? (*HOLMES takes the watch guardedly*) I have here a watch which some time ago came into my possession. Would you have the kindness to give me an opinion upon the character and habits of the late owner?

HOLMES takes a lens and gives it a perfunctory glance, then hands it back.

HOLMES There's hardly any data. It has recently been cleaned.

WATSON (*pleased with himself*) Yes!

HOLMES (*after a moment, reflectively*) Subject to your correction, I should say it belonged to your elder brother who inherited it from your father, H W, who has been dead many years. Your brother was a man of untidy habits. He was left with good prospects, but threw away his chances, lived for some time in poverty, with occasional short intervals of prosperity and, finally, taking to drink... he died. Yes, he died. That is all I can gather.

WATSON stares at the watch in bemusement, then with a note of asperity:

WATSON That is unworthy of you, Holmes. You have made enquiries into the history of my unhappy brother. Was it Stamford? And now you pretend to deduce this knowledge in some fanciful way. It is unkind and, to speak plainly, has a touch of charlatanism about it.

HOLMES (*chagrined*) My dear doctor, I crave your forgiveness. Viewing the matter as an abstract problem, I forgot how personal and painful a thing it might be to you. I assure you, however, that I never even knew you had a brother until you handed me that watch. (*WATSON stays silent, as HOLMES comes forward to demonstrate his deduction*) Well, look at it. You see it cut and marked, from the habit of keeping it next to coins and keys, in the same pocket. (*WATSON examines watch through a magnifying glass*) Thus he was careless. The watch is worth... fifty guineas? So he was well-provided for. And yet it carries the mark of the pawnbroker. Now, look at the scratches around the keyhole. What sober man's eyes could have scored those grooves? But you'll never see a drunkard's watch without them. And now it's in your possession, so the poor fellow must have died. I mean, where is the mystery in all this?

WATSON Ingenious.

HOLMES It's elementary. (*WATSON is humbled. HOLMES sinks deep into his chair with a note of exasperation*) What is the use of having brains in our profession? I know well that I have it in me to make my name famous, Watson. No man has ever lived who has brought the same amount of study and natural talent to the detection of crime which I have done. And what is the result? There are no crimes and no

criminals these days. (*Gets up and paces behind desk*) At most there is some bungling villainy with a motive so transparent that even a Scotland Yard official can see through it. Do you fence? (*He directs his violin bow towards WATSON's heart, playfully.*)
WATSON Playing rugby for Blackheath was my main sporting achievement.
HOLMES Bravo!

HOLMES exits. WATSON addresses the audience.

WATSON For the first week of so we had no callers and I concluded that Holmes was as friendless as I myself was. I soon found I was mistaken, however, when a stream of nondescript individuals began to arrive at odd hours. One little rat-faced, dark-eyed fellow was introduced to me as **Mr** Lestrade. He came three or four times. Then I remember there was a grey-haired seedy man, looking like a Jewish pedlar. He was closely followed by a slipshod elderly woman trailing a lame whippet.

HOLMES re-enters and busies himself at his desk.

HOLMES My clients, Watson. Would you mind leaving the room for a moment?

WATSON is waved away and continues to address the audience.

WATSON The next thing I noticed in those early days was that Holmes' ignorance was as remarkable as his knowledge.

HOLMES enters the new mood.

HOLMES Watson is extremely well read. Can quote you anything from contemporary literature...
WATSON Upon my quoting Thomas Carlyle, he enquired in the naivest way who he might be and what crime he had committed.

HOLMES He's very well informed about the Copernican theory.
HOLMES sits on couch with his back to WATSON.
WATSON My surprise reached a climax when I found that he was ignorant of the Copernican theory and the composition of the Solar system.
HOLMES Whereas I have no knowledge of such things.
WATSON That any human being in the nineteenth century should not be aware that the earth travelled round the sun appeared to me to be such an extraordinary fact that I could hardly believe it.
HOLMES You see, I consider a man's brain is like a little empty attic and you have to stock it with such furniture as you choose.
WATSON (*producing it from his pocket*) I drew up a list.
HOLMES (*surprised*) A list?
WATSON (*reads*) Knowledge of literature, nil. Philosophy, nil. Astronomy, nil. Politics, feeble. Botany, variable: well up in belladonna, opium and poisons generally.
HOLMES Only a fool takes in all the lumber.
WATSON Knows nothing of practical gardening. Knowledge of geology, practical, but limited: tells at a glance different soils from each other...
HOLMES It's a mistake to think that little attic room has elastic walls...
WATSON (*going doggedly on*) Knowledge of chemistry profound. Anatomy, accurate, but unsystematic.
HOLMES It's of the highest importance, therefore, not to have useless facts elbowing out the useful ones.
WATSON He is familiar with forty-two different

impressions of bicycle tyres. (*HOLMES laughs*) His knowledge of sensational literature, immense: he appears to know every detail of every horror perpetrated in the century. Plays the violin. Is an expert singlestick player, boxer and swordsman. Has a good practical knowledge of British law.

HOLMES You see, he lists all my virtues. Ignores his own.

And now a vigorous argument is being conducted.

WATSON But the Solar system!

HOLMES (*impatiently*) What the deuce is it to me? Now that you've told me I shall do my best to forget it!

WATSON Forget it?

HOLMES You say that we go round the sun! If we went round the moon it would not make a pennyworth of difference to me or to my work!

HOLMES strides upstage. The mood and the lights change. Music. With his back to the audience, HOLMES slips off his jacket, rolls up his shirt-sleeve, flexes his arm and 'injects' himself with cocaine. WATSON, seated with his newspaper, becomes aware and disturbed by his friend's action. As the drug takes effect, HOLMES lets out a small cry of relief. WATSON addresses the audience, quietly.

WATSON When first I discovered his habit, I was appalled. Being a medical man I knew the damage, which brought more peril to my friend than all the storm of his tempestuous life. And yet I found that I lacked the courage to protest. Again and again I registered a vow that I should deliver my soul upon the subject.

WATSON retires behind a book. HOLMES comes

furtively to the front of the stage and speaks privately his innermost thoughts.
HOLMES If it wasn't for Watson, I would have been dead within two years. A man needs a companion, he cannot sit alone... With his silent reproaches, his hurt looks, Watson controlled my addiction. And our walks, our conversations... the sheer breadth and enthusiasm of his mind on any manner of subjects kept me sane when the black fits were upon me. There never was a better friend. And I treated him abominably.

Exit HOLMES. WATSON is alone one summer evening. There are street sounds off, including a barrel organ. HOLMES enters energetically, humming the Wedding March.
HOLMES Watson! You'll be interested to hear I'm engaged to be married!
WATSON (*astonished*) Congratulations, my dear Holmes! To whom?
HOLMES The Milverton's housemaid. I needed information.
WATSON Oh, no... Surely you've gone too far!
HOLMES It was a most necessary step. I'm a plumber with a rising business. Escott, by name. I've walked out with her each evening and I've talked with her. Good heavens, those talks!
WATSON But the girl!
HOLMES You can't help it, Watson. You must play your cards as best you can when such a stake is on the table. However, I rejoice to say I have a hated rival who will certainly cut me out the instant my back is turned. What a splendid night it is!

HOLMES instantly asleep on the couch, legs up on the backrest. WATSON moves upstage. Summer evening sounds waft in from the street. WATSON talks to the audience.

WATSON There was only one woman in Holmes' life. Her name was Irene Adler. She was an opera singer from New Jersey, mistress to a king and quite one of the most ravishing beauties I have ever seen. *(Moves around stage left)* It was not that Holmes felt any emotion akin to love for her. For a trained reasoner to admit such intrusions might throw a doubt upon all his mental results. But when he speaks of her or when he refers to her photograph it is always under the honourable title of **the** woman.

HOLMES, still on couch, breaks the mood impatiently.

HOLMES Watson! These little records you keep of our cases... I cannot congratulate you upon them. Detection is, or should be, an exact science and should be treated in the same cold and unemotional manner. You have attempted to tinge them with romanticism, which produces much the same effect as if you worked a love-story or an elopement into the fifth proposition of Euclid.

WATSON *(clearly stung)* At the beginning I seem to remember you complimenting me on my honest observation.

HOLMES What you see and what your pen commits to the paper are two different things.

WATSON But would you have me describe you warts and all? Really, Holmes, I think this attack is quite unjustifiable. I have brought you in front of a wide public, who have demonstrated an insatiable appetite for your adventures and who keep clamouring for more. The very least my words have done is to bring you to the attention of the most powerful and the most in need. I have created your business for you! Would they know Sherlock Holmes, would they know Baker Street, without my publications? (*Turns away in indignation.*)

HOLMES (*mildly ashamed of himself*) Watson, my dear fellow, you are far too sensitive. If one cannot take a soupçon of criticism...

WATSON Can you, Holmes? Can you? Would you have me record your failures?

HOLMES What failures? (*Sits up and laughs, but WATSON is not amused*) Oh, I see, a joke! Watson, your value to me is inestimable. It was quite an unwarranted attack, which you're right to chide me for. When my brain is inactive I cannot help myself. How you've stuck it out these many years I shall never know.

WATSON I stick it out, old man, because, like you, I have to make a living.

The mood changes. Twilight. From the street a drunkard's shout. The cry of a woman. A police whistle. Footsteps running over cobbles. HOLMES fetches his top-hat and cane. He talks to the audience.

HOLMES Watson was right. The times are hard. We are reaching the end of a century where the rich get richer and the poor become ever more neglected. (*HOLMES is looking out of the window. WATSON is now dressed for outdoors.*) See, Watson... those ragged little street urchins... scarecrows... see their naked feet and their eager, expectant faces...

The chuff of a train. HOLMES and WATSON set

chairs opposite each other and sit. The lighting pulses regularly. They are in a train. HOLMES looks out of the window.

HOLMES   Watson! It's a very cheery thing to leave London by any of these lines which run high and allow you to look down upon the houses...

WATSON   There? Clapham? Those big isolated clumps, the board-schools?

HOLMES   Lighthouses, my boy! Beacons of the future! Capsules with hundreds of bright little seeds in each, out of which will spring the wiser, better England of the future.

A pause. Train noises die away. WATSON addresses the audience.

WATSON   It never ceases to amaze me. Holmes' unexpected breadth of vision... and his compassion. So unworldly is he – or so capricious – that he frequently refuses help to the powerful and wealthy where the problem makes no appeal to his sympathies, while he devotes weeks of most intense application to some humble client...

HOLMES   (*interrupting*) Watson...

WATSON turns to see HOLMES staring vacantly into the distance, deep in thought.

WATSON   Holmes? (*Taps him on shoulder. HOLMES looks up.*)

HOLMES   My dear fellow, I'm so sorry. I was miles away. Did you say something?

WATSON   You called me.

HOLMES   Did I? Well, well...

HOLMES relapses back into his private thoughts, alone in light, as the light fades on WATSON.

HOLMES   The cruelty of parents... to their children. My brother and I... forced... by accepted convention of upbringing... into such a frosted, trapped, inhibited dark corner... that we could not even communicate with each other. My father, absent, though never far away. We heard his step, his voice, but I scarcely exchanged a word with him before I was twelve. And mother, poor creature, starved of affection, yet I never saw her cry, not once. That vicious nurse! That house! The terror of silence...

The lighting changes to a dappled effect and they are walking in the park on another evening. Birdsong. A distant brass band playing Iolanthe.

HOLMES My ancestors were country squires, Watson, who appear to have led the life that is natural to their class. But none the less, my turn that way is in my veins and may have come with my grandmother who was the sister of Vernet, the French artist. Art in the blood is liable to take the strangest forms.

WATSON But how do you know that it's hereditary?

HOLMES Because my brother Mycroft possesses it in a larger degree than I do.

WATSON (*surprised*) I didn't know you had a brother, or relations of any sort. And to acknowledge a brother who is your superior...?

HOLMES (*laughs*) My dear Watson, I cannot agree with those who rank modesty among the virtues. When I say that Mycroft has better powers of observation than I, you may take it that I am speaking the exact and literal truth.

WATSON Does he use these powers for detective work?

HOLMES (*laughs*) If the art of deduction began and

	ended in reasoning from an armchair, my brother would have been the greatest criminal agent that ever lived. But he has no ambition and no energy.
WATSON	What is his profession then?
HOLMES	He works for the British government. (*They both laugh*) You might also say that occasionally he is the British Government!
WATSON	My dear Holmes!
HOLMES	It is the truth. He has the greatest capacity for storing facts of any man living. Ministers depend on him. Again and again his word has decided the national policy. He is Jupiter, Watson. And yet his temperament fixes him to a salary of a mere four hundred and fifty pounds a year... he will receive neither honour nor title, but remains the most indispensable man in the country. (*They are now in Pall Mall*) You see that doorway over there? It's the entrance to the Diogenes Club.
WATSON	I cannot recall the name.
HOLMES	Very likely not. There are many men in London, you know, who, from shyness or misanthropy, have no wish for the company of their fellows.
WATSON	(*smiles*) Yet are not averse to comfortable chairs or the latest periodicals?
HOLMES	Precisely. It is for their convenience that the Diogenes Club was founded and it now contains some of the most unsociable and unclubable men in London. No member is permitted to take the least notice of any other and no talking is allowed under any circumstances, save in the Strangers' Room. My brother was one of the founder members and I have myself found it a very

	soothing atmosphere.
WATSON	Is your brother there now? Am I permitted to meet him?
HOLMES	He is there every day from a quarter to five until twenty minutes to eight. (*Glances at watch*) Ah, it is five past. Another day, Watson.
WATSON	(*as they turn away*) He must have been a remarkable boy to have grown up with. Your household must have been extraordinarily alive with intellectual pursuit.
HOLMES	Oh, it was! (*Then privately*) How much one conceals from a friend... even a friend as close to me as Watson, how much one covers up... (*To WATSON*) It was, Watson, **vividly** alive!
WATSON	(*to audience*) It pleases me when Holmes feels he can talk frankly about himself. It removes the impression he gives to others, and to myself, I confess, at times, that he is an isolated phenomenon, a brain without a heart, as deficient in human sympathy as he is pre-eminent in intelligence.

WATSON exits - and returns to find HOLMES seated, busily engaged in a chemical experiment.

HOLMES	You come at a crisis, Watson. If this paper remains blue, all is well. If it turns red, it means a man's life. (*WATSON watches, fascinated, as HOLMES dips the litmus paper into the test-tube*) Hmm, I thought as much. I will be at your service in an instant. You will find tobacco in the Persian slipper. (*WATSON finds the tobacco as HOLMES completes his experiment, then turns*) A very commonplace little murder. You've got something

better, I fancy. You are the stormy petrel of crime, Watson. What is it?
WATSON I'm engaged to be married, Holmes. (*No emotion in Holmes' face*) To Mary Morstan...
HOLMES Ah! The heiress!
WATSON No, if you remember, she lost her fortune.
HOLMES (*a moment*) I am so pleased that you feel sufficiently recovered from your ordeals in Afghanistan to be able to contemplate matrimony.

HOLMES shakes WATSON warmly by the hand.
WATSON Well, you must take credit for that. It has been my acquaintance with you that has revived my spirits.
HOLMES (*a moment*) You'll be leaving Baker Street?
WATSON Well, naturally. You know that for some time I've been hankering after a return to medicine. I have managed to secure a practice.
HOLMES And a practice needs a wife.
WATSON (*cautious smile*) It helps.
HOLMES Excellent, my dear fellow, this calls for a celebration.
WATSON Shall I bring her over?
HOLMES Oh... (*He hadn't thought of it*) By all means. Yes, bring her over, Watson. We shall take the sweet young creature to Covent Garden. It's a Wagner night, I think.

WATSON starts to collect his things. Background music
WATSON I have naturally discussed with her my role as your biographer and frequent companion on your adventures, and she readily assures me that she has no objection to my continuing, if time permits...

HOLMES There are few women, Watson, in my experience, who would be so generous. I am fond of her already.
WATSON, *pleased with HOLMES' generous sentiments, leaves the stage and Baker Street. HOLMES, left alone on stage, calls after him, waving.*
HOLMES Good luck... (*The mood and lights change*) Mary Morstan is delightful. And very good for Watson, I've no doubt. (*Sits in WATSON's chair, hums a tune, makes finger movements for the violin and then flexes his arm, mindful of cocaine*) I am lost without my Boswell.
HOLMES is suddenly, intensely alone. WATSON returns downstage, to the audience.
WATSON During the first months of my marriage I have seen little of Holmes. My own complete happiness and home-centred interests are sufficient to absorb all my attention, while Holmes, who loathes every form of society with his bohemian soul, remains in our lodgings in Baker Street... (*Moves past HOLMES, who stays seated, oblivious to his presence*) alternating between cocaine and ambition, the drowsiness of the drug and the fierce energy of his own keen nature.
WATSON exits. The mood changes again: darker, menacing, intensified by sound. HOLMES becomes aware of another presence: the terrifying image of MORIARTY. His shadow stretches across the stage, street lit, in a London mist. HOLMES is alert, afraid.
HOLMES Professor Moriarty, I presume...? (*The shadow remains. Silence*) When the time is right, my friend, when the time is right...

The shadow moves away. WATSON's voice is heard.
WATSON Holmes? (*HOLMES stays perfectly still*) Can I be of assistance?
HOLMES Your presence might be invaluable.
WATSON You speak of danger. You are afraid of something?
HOLMES Well, I am.
WATSON Of what?
HOLMES Of air-guns.
This comes as a terrifying shriek from HOLMES. WATSON's voice has been in HOLMES' mind. Now his voice can be heard off-stage.
WATSON Holmes?
HOLMES (*with quiet relief*) My friend...
HOLMES rises from chair, as WATSON in outdoor clothes enters in natural light.
WATSON How are you, my dear fellow? I've brought you a cake. Mary baked it especially for you.
WATSON presents a cake tin. HOLMES peers inside, the briefest of glances. He puts in on the desk.
HOLMES How kind. And how is Mrs Watson?
WATSON She is extremely well, and sends you her compliments.
A pause.
HOLMES Watson... I think you know me well enough to understand that I am by no means a nervous man. At the same time it is stupidity, rather than courage, to refuse to recognise danger when it is close upon you. Might I trouble you for a match? (*WATSON lights HOLMES' cigarette and sees him staring ahead in a momentary trance - before he becomes aware of WATSON's presence again*) You have probably never heard of Professor Moriarty?
WATSON Never.

HOLMES goes upstage with a sudden surge of movement.

HOLMES   Ah, there's the genius and the wonder of the thing. The man pervades London and no-one has heard of him. That's what puts him on a pinnacle.

WATSON   What has he done?

HOLMES speaks with a fierce, rapid energy.
WATSON knows he is on cocaine.

HOLMES   He is the Napoleon of crime, Watson. The organiser of half that is evil and nearly all that is undetected in this great city. He is a genius, a philosopher, an abstract thinker. He has a brain of the first order. He sits motionless, like a spider in the centre of its web, but that web has a thousand radiations and he knows well every quiver of each of them...

WATSON can take no more. He interrupts angrily.

WATSON   What was it today? Morphine or cocaine?

HOLMES smiles, now suddenly languid.

HOLMES   Cocaine. A seven per cent solution. Would you care to try it?

WATSON   (*angrily*) No, indeed. My constitution has not got over the Afghan campaign yet. I cannot afford to throw any extra strain upon it.

HOLMES   Perhaps you're right, Watson. I suppose that its influence is physically a bad one. I find it, however, so transcendently stimulating and clarifying to the mind that its secondary action is a matter of small moment.

WATSON   But consider! Count the cost! Your brain may be aroused and excited, but it's a pathological and morbid process which involves increased tissue change and may, at least, leave a permanent weakness.

(*Takes HOLMES' pulse*) You know too, what a black reaction comes upon you. Surely the game is hardly worth the candle. Remember I speak, not only as one comrade to another, but as a medical man.

WATSON is kneeling beside HOLMES, his tone full of urgent concern. HOLMES responds furiously.

HOLMES My mind rebels at stagnation! Give me problems, give me work, give me the most abstruse cryptogram or the most intricate analysis and I am in my own proper atmosphere. I can dispense then with artificial stimulants. But I abhor the dull routine of existence, I crave for mental exaltation. That is why I have chosen my own particular profession or, rather, created it, for I am the only one in the world!

HOLMES exits fast, as the light fades. WATSON addresses the audience.

WATSON The strain caused by my friend's immense mental exertions in solving a number of cases, his dependence on drugs and his continuing obsession with Professor Moriarty gives me much cause for concern...

The lights come up on WATSON's study, late at night. A modest desk, cluttered with doctor's papers; a chair; a hat-stand. WATSON is seated at the desk, pipe alight, working late. HOLMES, dressed in long grey mac and trilby, enters quietly, unnoticed. His mood is calm, even apologetic. As WATSON now sees him, HOLMES looks like a strange, dark bird, with dull grey plumage.

HOLMES Ah, Watson... I hoped I might not be too late to catch you.

WATSON My dear fellow, pray come in.

HOLMES You look surprised, and no wonder! Relieved too, I fancy. You still smoke the Arcadia mixture of your bachelor days, then. There's no mistaking that fluffy ash on your lapel. (*WATSON looks down at his jacket, then brushes it with his hand. He sees HOLMES smiling at him*) Could you put me up for the night?
WATSON With pleasure.
HOLMES You told me that you had bachelor quarters for one and I see you have no gentleman visitor at present. Your hat-stand proclaims as much.
WATSON I shall be delighted if you'll stay.
HOLMES Thank you. I'll fill a vacant peg then. (*Puts his trilby on the stand and moves to front of desk. His attention is suddenly riveted to a mark on the floor*) Sorry to see that you've had the British workman in the house. He is a token of evil. Not the drains, I hope? (*Lies flat on his stomach on the floor, giving it his close attention*)
WATSON No, the gas.
HOLMES He has left two nail-marks from his boot on your linoleum, just where the light strikes it. (*Rises and, as WATSON makes to speak:*) No thank you, I had some supper at Waterloo. Is Mrs Watson in?
WATSON No... she is away on a visit.
HOLMES Indeed! You are alone?
WATSON Quite.
HOLMES Then it makes it easier for me to propose that you should come away with me for a week on the continent. (*Swiftly reclaims his hat and starts to go - turning back for a brief moment*) To Switzerland.
The light fades on HOLMES and he is gone. As WATSON steps forward to address the audience the

scene changes to the Reichenbach Falls. Against the backdrop a cascade appears, quickly spilling to engulf all the rear of the stage. The noise mounts in intensity.

WATSON   What took place on that fateful trip is well-recorded. It is not a subject upon which I would willingly dwell. But if there should be anyone here ignorant of that appalling event, then let me simply say that, near the Swiss village of Meiringen, at the Falls of Reichenbach, where the torrent, swollen by the melting snow, plunges into a tremendous abyss... Holmes finally confronted his arch-enemy Moriarty.

Thunder. Lightning. Cascading falls. WATSON turns towards them, shouting against the elements, his voice echoing.

WATSON   Holmes! Holmes!

Both HOLMES and MORIARTY must be plunging to their doom after a titanic struggle. Gradually the vision fades and the sounds die down. A last flicker of lightning and, in the ominous silence that follows, WATSON is seated at his desk alone, facing the audience.

WATSON   And I lost a friend - whom I regarded as the best and wisest man I've ever known.

HOLMES is discovered in his own light upstage, a shimmer of mist enveloping him.

HOLMES   What a lovely thing a rose is! There is nothing in which deduction is so necessary as in religion. It can be built up as an exact science by the reasoner. Our highest assurance of the goodness of Providence seems to me to rest in the flowers. All other things, our powers, our desires, our food, are all really necessary for our existence in the first instance. But this rose is an extra. Its smell and its colour are an embellishment of life, not a condition of it. It is only goodness which gives extras, and so I say again we have much to hope from the flowers.

The light fades on HOLMES and returns to WATSON, who raises his head from his hands.

WATSON Holmes?

HOLMES (*a disembodied voice*) I am here, my friend.

WATSON (*not hearing*) Holmes? Can I be of assistance?

His question is met by a faint echo of laughter from MORIARTY. WATSON is agitated. Alone. Knocks the ash from his pipe and moves forward to his armchair. He is distressed.

WATSON My sense of loss was compounded by the sudden, tragic death of my wife, Mary...

A pause

HOLMES (*disembodied*) Watson... work is the best antidote to sorrow.

WATSON gives a small acknowledgement to his absent friend, then, with a supreme effort, he pulls himself out of his desolate mood. He takes a stack of files from his desk and addresses the audience.

WATSON It can be imagined that my close intimacy with Sherlock Holmes has interested me deeply in crime. Among those unfinished cases is that of Mr James Phillimore who, stepping back into his own house to get his umbrella, was never more seen in this world. No less remarkable is that of the cutter *Alicia*, which sailed one spring morning into a small patch of mist from which she never again emerged, nor was anything further heard of herself or her crew. A third case, worthy of note, is that of Isadore Persana, the well-known journalist and duellist, who was found stark staring mad with a match box in front of him which contained a remarkable worm, said to be unknown to science. (*He pauses*) Ever since my friend's disappearance, three years ago, I've never failed to read with care the various problems which come before the public. I've even attempted more than once to employ his methods... though with indifferent success. (*Changes coat from jacket to white surgical coat*) One such case, recently, was the tragic murder of the Honourable Ronald Adair. While standing outside the house where the terrible event took place, I accidently struck against an elderly bookseller, spilling a pile of books from his hand. My attempted apology was greeted with a snarl of contempt...

Daylight now fills WATSON's study. WATSON confronts an elderly, deformed BOOKSELLER, his sharp, wizened face peering out from a frame of white hair. He has several old volumes wedged under his arm. He speaks in a strange, croaking voice.

BOOK'R I've a conscience, sir, and when I chanced to see you enter this house, I thought I'll just step in and see that kind doctor, and tell him if I was a bit gruff in my manner there was not any harm meant...

WATSON You make too much of a trifle. May I ask how you know who I am?

BOOK'R Well, sir, if it isn't too great a liberty, I am a neighbour of yours, for you'll find my little bookshop at the corner of Church Street, and very happy to see you, I am sure.

WATSON I'm afraid I'm extremely busy...

BOOK'R (*ignoring his protest*) Maybe you collect yourself, sir. Here's *British Birds* and *Catullus* and *The Holy War*...
He thrusts the books into WATSON's arms and stumbles into a chair.
WATSON I must ask you to leave.
WATSON exits briskly in search of help to remove the nuisance.
BOOK'R A bargain every one of them! (*He is on his feet again and moves behind the desk. He stoops down...*) Just what a man needs to complete his library.
WATSON returns.
WATSON I have a number of patients requiring urgent attention...
The BOOKSELLER straightens - and reveals himself to be HOLMES, now stripped of disguise.
WATSON Holmes?
HOLMES Ah, it's good to stretch oneself, Watson. It is no joke when a tall man has to take a foot off his stature for several hours on end.
He stretches himself and smiles. Flexes legs.
WATSON (*repeating*) Holmes!
WATSON faints backwards on to the floor.
HOLMES Watson! (*Peers over the desk at the prone figure, in utter amazement*) Watson? I owe you a thousand apologies. I had no idea you'd be so affected.

Music

CURTAIN

ACT TWO

We find HOLMES and WATSON once more in Baker Street. The furniture is covered in black dust sheets. HOLMES remains perfectly still, smoking a cigarette, behind his desk as WATSON makes a slow tour of the room, removing a dust sheet from the couch and blowing a cloud of dust from the chemicals table. A long moment.

WATSON (*in a calm voice*) Your books... papers... chemical equipment... violin...
HOLMES My brother, Mycroft, preserved them.
WATSON You chose Mycroft as your confidant, before me.
HOLMES Well, I had to confide in him in order to obtain the money I needed.
WATSON I could have sent you money.
HOLMES Oh, Watson...
WATSON I could have sold my practice.
HOLMES I wouldn't have dreamed of such a thing!
WATSON It isn't doing very well.
A pause. HOLMES is uncertain of WATSON's mood.
HOLMES Do take off your coat...
WATSON pointedly ignores the offer. He is still in a deep state of shock.
WATSON Where have you come from?
HOLMES I returned from France this morning, drawn by the news of this remarkable murder of the Honourable Ronald Adair. And at two o'clock this afternoon I found myself in my own armchair, only wishing that I could have seen my old friend in the other chair which he has so often adorned.
HOLMES sits in his old chair, throwing the dust

cloth to the floor. WATSON remains standing.

WATSON   And what did our housekeeper say when you walked through the door?

HOLMES   I'm afraid it threw our dear Mrs Hudson into a fit of hysterics. (*HOLMES stifles his amusement, then looks at WATSON, perplexed and for the first time, perhaps, a little unnerved by his stern countenance*) Are you not pleased to see me?

WATSON   Of course I'm pleased to see you. I'm overjoyed.

A pause.

HOLMES   (*warily*) Everything I did was for the best, Watson, I do assure you. There was a reason behind it. (*WATSON gives him a direct look, but still says nothing. HOLMES feels obliged to continue*) Many times... during the past three years... I have taken up my pen to write to you, but always I feared that your affectionate regard for me might tempt you to some indiscretion which would betray my secret.

HOLMES has risen, but WATSON walks abruptly from the room. HOLMES stares after him in amazement, then sits down again, fully aware now that he has misjudged the depth of his friend's feelings. After a moment WATSON re-appears. A further silence, then WATSON lets loose:

WATSON   Did you value our friendship as little as that? Whatever your reason I could have accommodated it. Just a word, a simple note. (*HOLMES tries to interrupt, but WATSON won't allow it*) Can there be any secret so precious that a man could allow his closest friend to believe he was dead for three whole years? (*A pause.*

WATSON *makes an effort to keep his emotions on a tight rein*) Consider the reverse. If I disappeared without word to you, would you not take it as a trifle unfeeling of me?
HOLMES I would have considered it uncharacteristic. I would have examined the data, and drawn conclusions.
WATSON Coldly.... without emotion?
A pause.
HOLMES It is clear that I have offended you deeply. If I explained what happened, would you perhaps find it in your soul to forgive me?
WATSON takes off his coat and hangs it up with deliberation.
WATSON I should like to hear what happened at Reichenbach.
HOLMES Then you shall. (*A moment as HOLMES composes himself*) Well now, about that chasm... I had no serious difficulty in getting out of it, Watson, for the very simple reason that I was never in it.
WATSON You were never in it?
HOLMES No, Watson, I never was in it. My note to you was absolutely genuine. I was convinced my life had reached its crisis... (*He pauses*) ... even before I perceived the sinister figure of the late Professor Moriarty standing on the narrow path which led to safety. He drew no weapon, but rushed at me and threw his long arms around me. He knew that his own game was up and was only anxious to revenge himself upon me. We tottered together upon the brink of the Falls. I have some knowledge, however, of baritsu or the Japanese system of wrestling, which has

> more than once been very useful to me. I saw him fall for a long way. Then he struck a rock, bounced off, and vanished into the abyss.

WATSON attentive. HOLMES has delivered all this between puffs of his cigarette, which he now puts out.

WATSON But the tracks... I saw with my own eyes that two went down the path and none returned.

HOLMES You saw the truth. But the instant the Professor disappeared, it struck me what a really extraordinary lucky chance Fate had placed in my way. I knew that Moriarty was not the only man who had sworn my death. There was Colonel Moran and at least three others. One of them would certainly get me. On the other hand, if all the world was convinced that I was dead... (*He pauses. WATSON remains listening impassively. Rashly, HOLMES attempts the teasing tone which has worked so well in the past, before his disappearance*) In your picturesque account of the matter, which I read with great interest some months later, you assert that the rocky wall behind and above me was sheer. That was not quite true. A few small footholds presented themselves and there was some indications of a ledge. If I returned along the wet path I should have left evidence of my survival.

WATSON You could have reversed your boots, as you've done on similar occasions.

HOLMES *pauses in astonishment at WATSON's astute observation.*

HOLMES I might, it is true have reversed my boots. But I decided to risk the climb. (*Pause*) It was not a pleasant business. The Falls roared beneath me. I am not a fanciful person, but I give you my word that I seemed to hear Moriarty's voice screaming at me out of the abyss. More than once tufts of grass came out in my hand or my foot slipped in the wet notches of the rock. I thought that I was gone. But at last I reached the ledge covered with soft green moss, where I could lie unseen in the most perfect comfort. There I was stretched, when you, my dear Watson, and all your following were investigating in the most sympathetic and inefficient manner the circumstances of my death. (*WATSON looks at him. This is the factor which most aggrieves him - that HOLMES was watching and allowing him to believe he was dead. HOLMES cannot hold his gaze, but is forced to continue in the same tone*)
At last, when you'd all formed your inevitable and totally erroneous conclusions, you departed for the hotel and I was left alone.

WATSON **You** were left alone...

HOLMES takes the force of this, then continues:

HOLMES Suddenly, a huge rock boomed past me and, looking up, I saw a man's head against the darkening sky. Another stone struck the ledge within a foot of my head. The meaning was obvious. (*He rises*) Moriarty had not been alone. I had no time to think of the danger, but slithered down from the ledge, took to my heels, did ten miles over the mountains in the darkness and, a week later, found myself in Florence, with the certainty that no-one in the world knew what had become of me.

A pause. The tale has come to rest, but where does it leave them? Scarcely reconciled.

WATSON Holmes...
HOLMES Yes?
WATSON Some time after my story of your death was published, I received a letter at my surgery. (*Sits on the arm of his chair, pushing the dust cloth to one side*)
It stated simply that Professor Moriarty was alive. That he had never met you at the Falls... was not in Switzerland at that time. That my account, therefore, was a tissue of lies.

A pause. HOLMES is intrigued.

HOLMES Did you keep this letter?
WATSON It's somewhere among my possessions.
HOLMES May I read it?

HOLMES has moved rapidly upstage and now returns to WATSON.

WATSON Of course. If I can lay my hands on it.
HOLMES One might reasonably assume it was written by a confederate, but what could be the purpose of informing you?
WATSON To discredit you?
HOLMES But if I'm dead...
WATSON Then your memory. The legend of Sherlock Holmes.
HOLMES Interesting. And how did you respond to this amazing letter?
WATSON I put myself in your shoes. I placed an advertisement in the *Times*, the gist of which was that you would be at a certain place at a certain hour and would welcome some proof... perhaps the

	Professor himself...
HOLMES	(*excitedly*) Excellent, my brave Watson, but how did you sign yourself?
WATSON	Some name, I forget. But the inference was clear.
HOLMES	And where was this rendezvous to be kept? For now I am convinced it was the work of Moriarty's gang.
WATSON	Here, in this room. Where else?
HOLMES	Here? But how piquant and clever of you.
WATSON	You have not asked me the question I expected. It would be logical to suppose that these rooms had been let to someone else.
HOLMES	(*conceding*) Watson, you have clearly been a diligent student... and have graduated with honours. Pray explain to me...
WATSON	Some weeks before, I found I had mislaid some medical notes. I concluded that I had left them here, among your papers. I called on Mrs Hudson and learnt that your brother, Mycroft, had instructed her to keep these rooms just as they were and had continued to pay the rent. It was my first intimation that you were still alive.

A pause.

HOLMES	And so you arrived at the appointed hour and sat in your old chair and, of course, no-one came.
WATSON	I sat for six hours. But how do you know that no-one came? Why should they not come?
HOLMES	Why should they? The letter was merely to put an idea into your head... that I had somehow lied to you and tricked you at Reichenbach.
WATSON	Well, if that was their scheme, it was a notable failure.

HOLMES So... you merely slept with your pistol under your pillow for a few months, then dismissed the whole fanciful notion from your head.
WATSON No... I went to see Mycroft. He received me, with a certain stiff cordiality, at the Diogenes Club.
HOLMES (*amazed*) Mycroft?
WATSON In the Strangers' Room. A very soothing atmosphere, if a little misanthropic. I put it to him quite bluntly. I said I thought you were alive and he knew of your whereabouts.

HOLMES is now seated in his chair and WATSON has moved to the front of the desk.

HOLMES And what did he say to that?
WATSON He twitched.
HOLMES But he was sworn to secrecy!
WATSON Oh, he was as good as his word on that point. He explained that he had preserved Baker Street as a memorial to you... on a whim. But your training me in the observation of human behaviour, Holmes, had not been in vain. Didn't you once tell me that human features are faithful servants to their emotions? It was not your brother's face, which showed no human emotion whatever, but a persistent tapping of the fingers of his left hand which drew my attention.

WATSON taps the fingers of his left hand on the desk top lightly.

HOLMES He is right-handed.
WATSON He had a large brandy and soda in his right hand. That never wavered. After a period of some – eleven minutes, he pleaded some urgent business and I left. I looked back through the window... he hadn't

>   shifted an inch.
> HOLMES (*joyfully, as he shakes hands warmly with WATSON*) My dear Watson, I am absolutely dumbfounded, and immensely proud of you.
> WATSON (*smiles*) Thank you, old man. But my visit failed to answer the burning question. I knew you were alive, but in what condition? And where? I did wonder... if you'd travelled East.
>
> *HOLMES has moved to stand by the couch.*
>
> HOLMES (*quietly*) You're right... I went to Tibet.
> WATSON Tibet?
> HOLMES I amused myself by visiting Lhassa. I spent some days with the Holy Lama.
> WATSON Was that instructive?
> HOLMES It was... illuminating. (*A moment*) You may have read of the remarkable explorations of a Norwegian named Sigerson, but I'm sure it never occurred to you that you were receiving news of your friend.
> WATSON Sigerson?
> HOLMES Sigerson.
> WATSON I remember now... that was the name I used in my advertisements. (*HOLMES gives WATSON a very sharp look, then recovers. Nothing WATSON does from now on will surprise him*) Where did you go after Tibet?
> HOLMES I passed through Persia, looked in at Mecca...
> WATSON (*amazed*) Mecca? You looked in at Mecca?
> HOLMES I then paid a short, but interesting, visit to the Khalifa at Khartoum, the results of which I have communicated to the Foreign Office. But to return to you, Watson... this burden you carried of my

WATSON existence... how did you deal with it?
WATSON After my visit to Mycroft, I felt certain I would receive a letter from you. And when I didn't... and months passed... and a year, then two... I was forced to the conclusion that you had met with some misfortune... had died... unnoticed and unmourned. When you came to me as that bookseller, I fainted because, quite frankly, I'd given you up.

Resumes his seat on the chair arm.
HOLMES Remarkable.
WATSON What happened after Khartoum?
HOLMES I spent some months in a research into the coal-tar derivatives, which I conducted in a laboratory at Montpellier in the South of France. Where I also heard of your sad bereavement.
WATSON How did you hear about Mary?
HOLMES Mycroft told me. He saw your announcement in the *Times*. My dear friend, I am so sorry. (*A pause*) There is no reasoning with the Fates. (*They seem at last to be on the brink of a genuine reconciliation - if Holmes can find it in himself to make the final move*) If it might seem to be a solution, your room is still here... just as it was. (*He glances at WATSON*) Shall I alert Mrs Hudson?

WATSON nods. HOLMES hurries off, upstage. WATSON breaks into a broad smile, snatches off the last dust cover from his own chair - and exits. Music as the lights fade to blackout. HOLMES is discovered lighting the lamp on his desk. He speaks privately.
HOLMES There are certain people to whom one cannot lie. My friend is one of them. And yet there are certain truths which cannot

44

be told... easily. (*A pause*) Sometimes one longs to be found out.

A pause. Then lights change to normal. WATSON enters briskly, shaking the rain off his umbrella.

WATSON   Wonderful news, Holmes!
HOLMES   What, my friend?
WATSON   I have sold my practice! A young doctor, named Verner has given me, with astonishingly little demur, the highest price I dared to ask.
HOLMES   Verner!
WATSON   Verner.
HOLMES   (*giving him a little help*) Verner... Vernet...

The penny drops for WATSON.

WATSON   Verner... Your grandmother... the sister of Vernet... the French artist...
HOLMES   No, no, no... a coincidence, my dear fellow. A distant relation...
WATSON   Holmes...

HOLMES laughs gleefully.

HOLMES   Well, now it is done! There is no more to be said on the matter.

WATSON sits in his chair and starts reading the newspaper. HOLMES hums and flexes his fingers, as for the violin. They are back in their old comfortable bachelor mood.

HOLMES   Anything in the newspaper?
WATSON   (*reading*) There's news of a revolution in South America... a possible war in Africa... an impending collapse of Government... (*He glances up*) Nothing to interest you.

A pause. Then HOLMES breaks the mood with sudden energy.

HOLMES   What do the public, the great unobservant public, who can hardly tell a weaver by his tooth or a compositor by his left thumb, care about the finer shades of

	analysis and deduction! (*He moves restlessly about the room*) When anno domini finally claims me, Watson, I have decided upon a life of philosophy, agriculture... and bee-keeping.
WATSON	Philosophy I understand after your sojourn in Tibet. Agriculture I question...
HOLMES	Oh, with a spud, a tin box, and a beginner's book on botany, there are instructive days to be spent...
WATSON	And bee-keeping?
HOLMES	One learns as much about human nature from the study of the bee, as from the study of people. Observation and deduction, Watson. Observation and deduction.
WATSON	Surely the one to some extent implies the other.
HOLMES	Watson, come to the window, quickly. (*WATSON joins him at the window*) Observe that young woman down there, the one who keeps glancing up at us... under the streetlamp, do you see? (*They both watch her for a moment, in silence*) Ah... she is moving away. (*WATSON moves back towards his chair*) Now then, what did you gather from her appearance. Describe it.
WATSON	Holmes...
HOLMES	No, no... take your time.

WATSON decides to give it a shot and starts with confidence.

| WATSON | She had a slate-coloured, broad-brimmed straw hat, with a feather... a brickish-red feather. Her jacket was black. Her dress was brown, with a little purple plush at the neck and sleeves. Her gloves were greyish and were worn through at the |

	right forefinger.
HOLMES	Her boots?
WATSON	Her boots... I didn't observe. But she had small round hanging gold earrings, and had a general air of being fairly well-to-do in a vulgar, comfortable, easy-going way.
HOLMES	(*applauds, laughs*) 'Pon my word, Watson, you are coming along wonderfully. You've really done very well indeed. It's true that you've missed everything of importance, but you've hit upon the method, and you have a quick eye for colour. What you failed to deduce was that she was short--sighted... the dint of a pince-nez on either side of her nose... she had come out in odd boots and she had written a note in haste before leaving.
WATSON	A note?
HOLMES	You observed that her right glove was torn, but you did not notice that both glove and forefinger were stained with violet ink. Amusing, but very elementary.

His mood has suddenly changed and WATSON feels a moment of concern for him: decides to humour him with philosophy.

WATSON	Life is infinitely stranger than anything which the mind of man could invent, don't you think, Holmes?

The lights dim to reflect HOLMES private thoughts:

HOLMES	Yes... if we could fly out of that window hand in hand, hover over this great city, gently remove the roofs, and peep in at the strange coincidences, the plannings, the cross-purposes, the wonderful chain of events, working through generations, and leading to the most outre results, it would make all fiction, with its

conventionalities and foreseen conclusions, most stale and unprofitable. (*HOLMES puts his hand to his head, whispers*) Irene... Irene... I can still catch the fragrance of her scent...

Soft music. WATSON comes to HOLMES.

WATSON Are you all right, old man?

HOLMES (*breaking the mood*) Bored, Watson! Bored! For all this talk of rooftops and windows and women... London has become a singularly uninteresting city since the death of the late, lamented Professor Moriarty! (*HOLMES once more returns to a reasonable mood, but WATSON is becoming worried for his state of mind*) Do you recall Miss Irene Adler?

WATSON Of course. How could I forget?

HOLMES Sometimes I believe I can hear her enchanting voice.

WATSON is amused by this unexpected revelation.

WATSON She's a married woman, Holmes.

HOLMES She was... She died alone in Biarritz (*He glances at WATSON*) Mycroft saw a small announcement in the *Times*.

WATSON (*a moment*) Do you still carry her photograph?

HOLMES It may well be somewhere amongst the jumble of my papers. (*He throws some papers about*) We must lay to rest the ghosts of our past, Watson. All of them! (*He pauses, realising suddenly that he has invoked a memory of Mary Watson*)
Oh, my dear fellow... how tactless of me. I had no wish to bring back your memories in such a way. I was... selfishly... exorcising my own.

WATSON (*a brief smile*) There's no damage.

He returns to his chair and picks up the paper.

HOLMES Watson... did you know that Moriarty has a brother who is a station master in the West Country?
WATSON No. But it doesn't surprise me to hear that trains run in the family, so to speak.
HOLMES (*surprised*) Really?
WATSON Was it not Moriarty who drove the engine past us on Canterbury Station... when we were endeavouring to escape the country?
HOLMES (*remembering*) It was, indeed.
WATSON And I know, of course, of Colonel James Moriarty who defended the memory of his brother in the press after the tragedy of Reichenbach was made known.
HOLMES (*truly surprised*) Colonel **James** Moriarty?
WATSON Well, good heavens, it was those infamous letters which prompted me to publish what I believed at the time to be the truthful account.

Pause. HOLMES thoughtful. He picks up a churchwarden from the desk and turns to face WATSON.

HOLMES Watson... whom do you see in front of you?
WATSON I see you... my friend... Sherlock Holmes...
HOLMES And who am I now?

HOLMES adopts the stooped posture of the bookseller.

WATSON That bookseller fellow...

HOLMES is now in the posture of the drunken loafer.

HOLMES Who now?
WATSON One of your loafers and idlers... (*HOLMES changes again: WATSON chuckles*) That's the foolish clergyman... I recognise him.
HOLMES And now? (*Music. HOLMES adopts the unmistakeably sinister pose of ex-Professor Moriarty. WATSON stiffens. As MORIARTY HOLMES says:*) You evidently don't know me.

WATSON On the contrary, I think it is fairly evident that I do.
HOLMES It has been an intellectual treat to duel with you, Mr Holmes, but I know every move of your game. You hope to beat me. I tell you that you will never beat me. If you are clever enough to bring destruction upon me, rest assured that I shall do as much to you.
HOLMES moves, snake-like, around WATSON's chair, then upstage, where he freezes and collapses, just as WATSON rushes to stop him hitting the floor.
WATSON (*alarmed*) Holmes!
Music. Lights change. WATSON guides the stricken HOLMES to the couch. HOLMES is delirious.
HOLMES Oysters! Oysters! Shall the whole bed of the ocean be overrun by them? Are there not natural enemies which limit the increase of these creatures?
WATSON puts a rug over him and goes quickly for medicine. HOLMES comes round and sees WATSON returning.
HOLMES Watson, leave me.
WATSON I have no such intention. You are sick, I must treat you.
HOLMES If I'm to have a doctor, let me at least have someone in whom I have confidence.
WATSON You have none in me?
HOLMES In your friendship, certainly. But facts are facts, Watson... you are only a GP... with very limited experience and mediocre qualifications.
WATSON That is unworthy of you, Holmes – and shows me very clearly the state of your nerves...
HOLMES (*weak, but furious*) Shall I demonstrate your ignorance? What do you know, pray, of Tapanuli fever? What do you know of

WATSON   the black Formosa corruption?
WATSON   I have never heard of either.
HOLMES   There are many problems of disease, many strange pathological disorders in the East...

WATSON forces HOLMES to take the medicine.

WATSON   Though you may show no confidence in me... in the past few days, I have brought Sir Jasper Meek and Penrose Fisher... and Doctor Aintree, the greatest living authority on tropical diseases... all to your bedside...

HOLMES begins slowly to recover, raises himself to wrap the rug around his shoulders. He is still weak.

HOLMES   My dear Watson, I do most sincerely apologise. I had no wish to alarm you. I fear that I am beyond the medical pale, Watson.

WATSON   (*frustrated*) For the very good reason that you have no diagnosable symptoms!

HOLMES   You are right. I have devised my own remedy... it requires not your medical skills which I am sure are more than adequate, but your powers of deduction and logic. Will you assist me?

WATSON   (*taking his arm and leading him back to a chair*) In any way I can.

HOLMES   Thank you. My illness comes from the brain... and nor is cocaine the answer, I have tried it. Only the brain has the cure.

WATSON   Just tell me what you wish me to do.

HOLMES   I propose to offer you... the hypothesis... that Professor Moriarty did not exist. That I invented him.

He looks up. A pause.

WATSON   (*a short laugh*) My dear Holmes...

HOLMES (*silencing him*) You must challenge it at every point, let nothing escape you. I have laid in your favourite claret and the tobacco is in the slipper. Are you game for it?

WATSON Why, yes, of course. If you insist...

HOLMES summons up a supreme act of mental will and begins his story.

HOLMES So. It was in the summer of '87 that the idea first came to me. It may have sprung from one of my black fits, quite probably it did, I forget... but its practicality was purely logical. I am an acknowledged expert in all matters criminal. If I could create a master... (*He pauses, then continues with a supreme effort of will*) ... a master mind which could draw to it, like the spider, all the nefarious flies, into its web, then how much easier it would be to keep my own finger on the pulse. (*WATSON is listening intently, as HOLMES moves slowly across and sits in WATSON's chair*) I took my plan to Mycroft in the Diogenes Club, and he was entranced. He saw it as a moral imperative, an altruistic gesture... and immediately offered his services, without quibble.

WATSON May I interrupt?

HOLMES Please do.

WATSON Moriarty is known by others. I have seen his biography in publications. His education is listed, his clubs...

HOLMES Most of the information you received came from my own lips, and you were naturally too trusting to cross-check. But there **are** facts known about his remarkable career, which can be verified,

              for the very simple reason that I put them about myself. Shall I continue?
WATSON (*shaken*) By all means.
HOLMES I took the name from an old Mathematics Professor I had known at University, a dear, sweet man, as far removed in temperament from my creation as anyone could ever be.
WATSON Was he then the author of that book...?
HOLMES *The Dynamics of an Asteroid.* The very same.
WATSON But I remember you saying that it touched such rarefied heights of pure mathematics that no man in the scientific press was capable of criticising it?
HOLMES For the simple reason that no man ever read it. It was the poor man's life work and was totally obscure and impenetrable.
WATSON Where did you base your operation?
HOLMES Here, in Baker Street.
WATSON Here!
HOLMES You remember those odd occasions when I asked you to retire to your room for an hour or so...?
WATSON You were Moriarty here? But all the world knows that Holmes lives here!
HOLMES A small conceit... that Moriarty occasionally played the cuckoo... in Holmes' nest. (*WATSON marvels at HOLMES' cheek*) You may be surprised to hear that it was only necessary for me to appear in public as Moriarty twice – once in the Grill Room at the Savoy Hotel and once in the waiting room at Crewe Station... I think...
WATSON (*doggedly*) We saw him together, on the station platform at Canterbury...
HOLMES That was my brother Mycroft.

WATSON Moriarty's brother, the Colonel, who wrote defending him...
HOLMES Mycroft again, on a whim.
WATSON And Reichenbach?
HOLMES Did you not receive some letter to the effect that the Professor never was in Switzerland?
WATSON Mycroft wrote it?
HOLMES No, that was almost certainly written by Colonel Moran, his confederate.
WATSON You told me once that Moriarty supplied Moran liberally with money. That surely cannot have been your own money, Holmes?
HOLMES It was not! I simply invented that, for a little amusement.
WATSON (*sudden anger*) If you invented him for your amusement, it was at my expense! I really don't think I can believe anything you ever say again.

WATSON *is genuinely disturbed. What if HOLMES is telling the truth? There is something horribly plausible developing.*
HOLMES We are only play-acting, my friend.
WATSON I fail to see where it is leading us.
HOLMES You will. I beg you to continue.
WATSON The Professor was seen at the hotel at Meiringen.
HOLMES My third appearance – a brief one, merely for local colour.
WATSON And Colonel Moran... above you, at the Falls. If you were alone...
HOLMES That, ironically, was fact. I had intimated to Moran that I was to meet Sherlock Holmes for the final resolution. Assuming that his master had perished, Moran tried to avenge him.

A pause.

WATSON The airgun with which Colonel Moran shot Ronald Adair. You told Inspector Lestrade that it was ordered by Moriarty from the German mechanic, Von Herder. Was it you who commissioned that?
WATSON stares at HOLMES in utter disbelief.
HOLMES (*evenly*) I have done things in many areas of my life, Watson, which at the time I believed were for the greater good, but which have taken some unfortunate victim along the way. (*A pause*) You must take me as you find me.
WATSON I consider that an abhorrent answer, Holmes! I cannot accept it!
HOLMES Do you wish me to enumerate the lives saved by my unique position?
WATSON I cannot accept it! Any of it!
HOLMES So be it.
WATSON is staring at his friend, who seems both forlorn and indifferent.
WATSON There is only one question which concerns me before we abandon this fool's journey.
HOLMES I am ready for it.
WATSON If you did indeed create this monster, then what prompted you to destroy him?
A pause.
HOLMES I could not live with him. It was either him or me. And I had contemplated both solutions. (*He looks directly at WATSON*) When the moment came, I decided to give myself one final chance.
WATSON Tibet...
HOLMES I thought I might find something there.
WATSON And what did you find?
HOLMES rises to his feet.
HOLMES Intolerable loneliness. And no solutions. And nothing to exercise my mind. Beyond

the arid abstractions of philosophy. They are a sweet and gentle people, Watson. Seldom vindictive, and therefore no crimes, no mysteries to solve. Once in a village, I thought I stumbled upon one – a brutal and motiveless dismembering of a goat. I applied my usual methods. My Watson was a bright-eyed child of twelve, the son of one of the Elders of the village. In the course of a single afternoon, he presented me with seven clues, all of which I missed, and he had the culprit gibbering his confession by nightfall. Very salutary. I was out of my element. I missed the thronging streets of London, and your companionship.

A pause. WATSON is now seated in HOLMES' chair. HOLMES moves round the room.

WATSON I, too... was out of my element.

HOLMES An elementary diagnosis which the Lama made. There is nothing here for you, return to Watson, said the Holy Lama. Then he added but there is a price you must pay. The man you killed has not left you. Your friend and your enemy are one.

WATSON (*a short laugh*) Now I am Moriarty?

HOLMES (*smiles*) There was a language problem. But his meaning was clear. You cannot have Watson without Moriarty. You cannot have Moriarty without Watson. And without both of them, there is no Holmes. The three of us are inextricably bound, you see.

WATSON (*steadily*) But Moriarty is dead. You killed him.

HOLMES Oh, yes. I killed him. At Reichenbach. As you so faithfully recounted.

WATSON That is the truth?
HOLMES is back in WATSON's chair. He speaks with quiet desperation.
HOLMES The absolute truth. You do believe me?
WATSON I have always believed you.
HOLMES accepts this gratefully.
HOLMES It was the continuing presence of that malignant brain in mine which caused my collapse and my unruly behaviour... (*A moment of silence - as we see Holmes give way to his emotions, publicly, for perhaps the only time in his life.*) For which once again, Watson, I crave your forgiveness. (*Rises to cross the room to his desk with a rush of furious energy and anger.*) My hypothesis was a quixotic act to rid myself... I would always stake my cold, precise mind against any deviltry... I do believe my hypothesis would have stood the test of pure reasoning... had not you typically, my friend, thrown morality into the works. There could be no side-stepping that.
HOLMES stands behind WATSON who has not moved. But WATSON now detects a change of mood in HOLMES.
WATSON Well, perhaps it served its purpose. You seem recovered... released. And as for your health I can only pray there will be no successor to Moriarty.
HOLMES (*exasperated*) You have missed the point entirely, Watson. There must be a successor! For my sanity! I am comforted to know that he is that many-headed Hydra. As soon as one head is cut off, another grows in its place. It is essential to our well-being, Watson, that there will

always somewhere be a Moriarty among us.

WATSON remains calm, sticking to his guns.

WATSON I hardly think you'll find many decent citizens agreeing with you. Can we not feed off the stories beneath the roofs... of ordinary people, peep in at the strange coincidences, the plannings, the cross-purposes, the wonderful chain of events... leading to the most outré results?

HOLMES (*amused*) Did you say that? I seem to hear my voice.

WATSON Your voice, my voice... they are inextricably bound, aren't they, Holmes?

HOLMES You are developing an unexpected vein of pawky humour, Watson, against which I must learn to guard myself. Will you be entrusting to print these secrets we've shared this evening... verbatim?

WATSON I shall, as always, respect your wishes, Holmes, and select... and hone... and transpose... and omit... and, I hope, fulfil the expectations of your adoring public.

WATSON has risen and moved past HOLMES.

HOLMES I am must humbly grateful. Thank you.

WATSON offers HOLMES back his chair. HOLMES sits in the lotus position, closing his eyes in meditation. Then he extends his hand towards WATSON.

HOLMES You are the one fixed point in a changing world.

WATSON fills his pipe before acknowledging:

WATSON Thank you, Holmes.

Soothing music. Then a doorbell rings, offstage. Watson looks at his watch, not expecting callers.

WATSON Who can that be?

HOLMES Unless I am mistaken, Watson... it's a

client.
He raises his arms upwards, like a man reborn.
WATSON shares his delighted laughter.

CURTAIN

MURDER TONIGHT!

Rehearsed Improvisations on a Theme, by Ian Wilkes

pb   5.5 x 8.5 $10   ISBN 0-88734-904-8

A collection of improvisations aimed specifically at public showings and participation, where cast blends with audience to solve a mystery – usually a murder! An entertaining improvisational tool, and ideal for a dinner-theatre setting, a hotel lobby, a private party – even the traditional stage. Many of these events are staged as weddings, fancy-dress balls, medieval feasts and even large parties, but by far the most popular form is the "Murder dinner." Rehearsed improvisations, when presented for and with the public, are unpredictable and always exciting entertainment. As author Ian Wilkes says, "What happens during any one performance is in the lap of the gods."

THREE COSTUME PLAYS FOR WOMEN

Three delightful one-act period pieces by Ian Wilkes, Marjorie Wing, and Norman Holland. Cast of twenty-two females (doubling if desired).

pb   5.5 X 8.5 $7(£7)   ISBN 0-88734-914-5

The collection includes: *QUEEN VICTORIA IS AMUSED*, when visited by the wife of resigning Prime Minister Gladstone, who is determined to win some expression of royal esteem for her controversial husband; *VOTES FOR WOMEN*, as Stella Hastings and her compatriots plot a campaign of genteel civil disobedience for suffrage; and *THE MORNING OF THE BALL*, a wry look into the home of a "happy" family who are deep in the midst of preparations to snare husbands for their daughters – whether they want them or not. A truly wonderful collection of female roles in colorful settings that will keep audiences intrigued and entertained.